Injury Time

MICHAEL HARDCASTLE

Illustrated by Chris Leishman

MACDONALD YOUNG BOOKS

Chapter One

"So what's wrong with you today, Joe?" Miss Tolley asked near the end of maths.

"Nothing, Miss Tolley," Joe replied automatically. Then he blinked and added "What d'you mean?"

"That bandage on your left hand," she pointed. "What happened?"

"Oh that!" Joe said, brightening. "I was doing a scissors kick to score a goal – that means you're up in mid-air – so it was a long way down. I hurt my hand when I put it out to save myself."

"That's a new one," smiled Miss Tolley, wondering if the story were true.

"So did you score, then?" called out Sam from the other side of the classroom.

"Er, no. The goalie knocked it down – at the second attempt," replied Joe, almost as if he'd rehearsed the answer. "It was dead on target, you see. Real power. That's why the goalie couldn't hold it."

"Couldn't you have got up faster and stabbed the ball in?" Sam went on.

"I probably would have if their full-back hadn't stood on my hand," Joe explained. "It was deliberate. He knew I was their biggest threat. They wanted a chance to put me out of the game."

"Of course," Sam said sarcastically. Several boys laughed, though none of the girls did.

Amy smiled at Joe and got a half-smile in return. Then she turned to her friend Emma. "Joe's really good, you know," she whispered. "When he's fit he looks terrific on the ball. Oh, and he's brilliant at passing. I should know, I got a great pass when we were training with the Swifts last week."

"Oh, really?" said Emma, who wasn't the slightest bit interested in football.

"Yes, and soon Joe and I are going to be team-mates," Amy added. By now Emma had become bored with the conversation and was flicking pieces of paper at Sanjay.

The shrill sound of the bell signalled the end of school.

"Put up your chairs now, class," said Miss Tolley. "See you all tomorrow."

Chapter Two

In the staffroom, Miss Tolley was still wondering about Joe's story. "What is it with Joe Reith?" she asked. "Is he just injury-prone, or what? I mean, practically every week he's got a new bandage or plaster, usually in a different place from the last time. It was his hand today. Yet he says he hurt it playing football. You wouldn't say he was a weakling, would you? Quite sturdy and fit?"

Mr Fletcher shrugged. "Well, it's true he does seem to suffer a lot. Doesn't actually break anything, though," he grinned. "Well, not yet! And I'm sure he'd tell us if he did."

Miss Tolley frowned. "But is he really any good as a player? The rest of the class seem to have mixed feelings about him as far as I can tell."

"He's definitely got bags of talent. He just doesn't always show it. It could be a stamina problem, come to think of it. I mean, he rarely lasts an entire match. Yes, maybe you've hit on something there. Should we mention it to the new coach?"

"I don't know. Perhaps we're just interfering," Miss Tolley said. "Let's see what happens in the next match."

Chapter Three

"Come on, Joe, get stuck in!" yelled Ivan Jones as his players got involved in a goal-mouth skirmish. "Get that ball and clear it! Clear it!"

Joe heard the call but had no intention of acting on it. He was supposed to be playing in defence and he loathed it. He was a striker and should always be a striker; his job was to score goals, not to stop them. But Ivan Jones, the Swifts' new coach, had some weird ideas about training.

One of them was to play people on different positions. "Then you'll find out how opponents are trying to deal with you," he claimed. But Joe still found it difficult.

This training session at Castle Playing Fields was hard work for everyone. The players were going flat out to impress their new coach so that he'd be sure to pick them for his first full game as boss. As for Ivan Jones, he was determined to demonstrate that he had lots of energy and new ideas. He was already working out who he wanted in the team against Dinting Redsox on Sunday. It wouldn't be a bad idea, he decided, to spring a few surprises. That would make everyone sit up and take notice.

"Jonathan, take a break," he yelled to the tall midfielder who'd just made a fierce tackle but still failed to win the ball. "Come and swap bibs with Amy here." Then he turned to the girl with short blonde hair who was standing close by. She had one foot resting on the bench where the subs usually sat. "Go on and do your best, girl," he told her. "My spies tell me that you can play a bit when you get a chance. This is your chance to twinkle like the brightest star!"

"Thanks, Mr Jones," said Amy happily. She hadn't expected to be playing this evening because she was sure the coach would just watch the boys. Now, if she played her best, she could win a place in the line-up against Dinting Redsox, one of the best teams in the Sunday League.

Almost at once she picked up a stray ball, turned cleverly in a half-circle to avoid one opponent and nutmegged another by slipping the ball between his legs as he tried to stop her. Spotting Joe in a space on the right, she fed him a perfect pass.

"Well done, girl, well done!" the coach sang out. "That's the way I want it."

Amy's spirits soared. Although she wished he wouldn't call her "girl" she was thrilled with the praise. The Swifts' previous coach had played her for only one full match, even though he'd told her privately she was as good as any of the boys. Perhaps Mr Jones was different and genuinely believed in choosing the best players for his team whether they were boys or girls. He certainly seemed willing to give people a fair chance.

Chapter Four

Joe, pleased with Amy's pass, darted forward, eager to impress the boss too. He neatly skipped past an opponent, slipped the ball sideways to Dan, called for an instant return, and got it. By now he was on the edge of the penalty area. The goal was in his sights and he couldn't resist a shot. So he let fly with his left foot. But the ball went straight to the goalkeeper.

"Complete waste of time that was, Joe," yelled Ivan Jones. "You're supposed to be a defender, not an attacker. So stay BACK!"

Amy shot Joe a sympathetic smile, but Joe wasn't upset, he was annoyed. He'd guessed he'd be told off. But if he didn't get the ball into the net how was he going to persuade a new coach to play him as the main striker? Joe knew he wouldn't get anywhere playing in defence, he'd had to do something to catch the coach's attention. Like Amy, he desperately wanted to play in the match on Sunday. He couldn't get through a weekend without football.

His mind was wandering when he suddenly heard a call of "Yours, Joe!" from Amy. Another perfect pass. Another fast, weaving run with the ball. Another golden chance of a goal. And this time he drove the ball into the net, giving the goalie no earthly chance of a save.

In the moment of scoring, however, Joe went
down under a crunching tackle from Jack. And
he stayed down, for the pain in his right calf was
awful. Ivan Jones guessed that he might be hurt
and, after blowing his whistle to stop the game,
he dashed on to the pitch. Amy watched
anxiously as the coach prodded and massaged
Joe's calf and then applied a pain-killing spray.
To Joe's surprise, the coach didn't criticize him
for going forward, but neither did he praise
his goal.

"Just take it easy – see how it goes," he told Joe. "Want to come off?"

"I think I'd better," Joe grimaced. It was a long time since any one had been this concerned about him. It felt strange. After that he walked around fairly carefully until the coach decided they'd all done enough training for one night.

He told them they'd all played well, but he needed to think about who to put in against Redsox on Sunday.

Nobody could get him to say any more. They would just have to wait and see.

As Amy and Joe walked home together, Amy asked "Joe, why did you leave the pitch after scoring? You often do it. And your leg doesn't hurt any more, does it?"

"How d'you know that?"

"Because you're not limping now, or anything. So why didn't you get back on the pitch and score some more?"

"Because the coach will remember what I did if my last touch was to score a goal," Joe explained.

Amy thought about this for a few moments and then said "Maybe, but they'll also remember you were injured. That's what people already say, you know. They say, 'Oh Joe, yeah, he's always crying off because he's injured.' Honestly, I've heard them."

Joe didn't say anything, just looked at his feet and scowled. Amy was afraid he wouldn't talk to her anymore but when they got to her house, she asked him if he'd like a drink and he said yes. Amy's mum fussed over him because she knew Amy liked him. They talked about football and Joe was surprised by how much Mrs Baxter knew about the game. He felt a twinge of envy as Mrs Baxter asked questions about how Amy had played. Amy's room was a shrine to football – wall posters, action pictures, scarves, signed photographs, and two full autograph books. Amy's mum seemed to be just as interested in football as Amy was.

Joe stayed talking to them both for a long time. He liked Mrs Baxter. When he was leaving, Amy said "You don't like coaches, do you? Why?"

"Don't trust 'em," was the instant reply. When Amy tried to get him to explain, all he would say was "I'll tell you one day."

Chapter Five

It was just before the kick-off against Dinting Redsox. As he spoke, Ivan Jones jabbed at the air with a finger to emphasize the importance of his words. "A striker has to have courage, loads of it," he was saying. "Sometimes you have to push yourself through the pain barrier. But it's worth it to score a goal. And, as you know, matches are won or lost, on goals."

Joe thought the coach was talking just to
him but Tom, his co-striker, kept nodding his
agreement. Tom was Joe's rival in the Swifts'
squad and Joe always wanted to out-score him.
Now Mr Jones was pointing to a sticking plaster
on Joe's thigh. "That's not a legacy of that tackle
I treated you for at training, is it?" he asked.

"Er no, the neighbour's dog tried to eat a
chunk of my leg," Joe said "It's still a bit sore,
but nothing serious."

"But you're fit, Joe, aren't you? Fully fit for this match?" Mr Jones wanted to know. "Can't do with half-fit players against a team like the Redsox. They're dynamite."

"I'm fine, Coach, don't worry," Joe said. He was aware that Amy was watching him but he avoided her eye. All the same, he was glad she was playing because she'd send him her best passes. She was a brilliant player and really tough. She never avoided a tackle.

Amy really needed that attitude because the Redsox were as hard as concrete. Although they played skilful passes that often surprised their opponents, they mixed their skills with lots of aggression. It made no difference to them that Amy was a girl and, shortly after kick-off, she

suffered a blockbusting tackle that earned the offender a yellow card. Joe saw the tears in her eyes as she clutched her knee and was treated by Mr Jones. But as soon as she could, she was on her feet and carrying on with the game. "Well done, girl," sang out Ivan Jones from the touchline when she slid in for a tackle. She merged with the ball and fed Joe one of her precision passes.

Joe had to skip around another fierce tackle, which showed the yellow card hadn't clipped Redsox's style. With a burst of speed he dashed past two more opponents and then flicked the ball sideways to Tom, his co-striker. Even before Tom could bring the ball under control he was mown down by Redsox's solidly-built captain.

It was another foul and the referee was furious. After showing another yellow card, he made the Redsox team gather round while he warned them about foul play. On the touchline, Ivan Jones nodded his approval.

Chapter Six

In spite of their superior skills, Redsox couldn't manage to get a goal. But neither could the Swifts. Both Tom and Amy were limping, but refusing to leave the pitch for extra treatment or a rest. Joe was working harder then he'd ever done in a match and was enjoying himself. What's more, the coach kept singing out his praises. "How d'you feel?" Joe asked Amy at half-time, as they ate bananas for energy.

"It hurts, but I can live with it," she grimaced. "I need the coach to keep choosing me for the team. Anyway, Tom seems worse off than me."

The game was just as rough in the second half. Dinting Redsox were desperate for a goal and their supporters roared their approval at every tackle and every attack they made. Once again, Tom went down and this time his opponent got the red card and was sent off.

Even with one player down, the Redsox kept up their fierce efforts to win the ball and put it in the net. Joe, under orders from the coach to help out the defence, took a kick on the thigh and a jabbed heel on his instep. Both times, the offender made sure the ref wasn't looking.

Joe gasped when he tried to run and had to give up until the pain eased. "Don't weaken now, Joe Reith!" yelled the coach for everyone to hear. He had meant to be encouraging, but Joe thought he was unfair. Until then, he'd given his team everything. Now it seemed to him that nobody was going to get anything out of the game. It would be a draw, but at least the Swifts would get a point against the League's top team.

Then Amy, battling as if her life depended upon it, came out of a scramble with the ball and slid it temptingly in front of Joe. He was on the edge of the Redsox penalty area. Joe immediately swivelled, ignored the pain in his foot, whipped past a defender and fired a raging shot into the top of the net. The goalkeeper didn't even see the ball pass him. Ivan Jones was jumping up and down on the touchline and the supporters were yelling and cheering. Joe, the hero, was sitting on the ground, nursing his foot.

"Terrible pain!" he gasped as Amy tried to haul him to his feet. Moments later, the coach came to help him off the pitch. But now Mr Jones was scowling. He didn't offer one word of praise. "You should stay on just for nuisance value," he said grimly. "There's only about a minute left."

It was just long enough for Dinting Redsox to grab the equalizer. Almost from the re-start, they swept upfield and won a corner. When the ball swung in towards the goalmouth, the keeper jumped, failed to collect it and an attacker somehow jabbed it into the empty net.

"You see what I mean, Joe!" fumed the coach. "I needed to pack the penalty area with bodies. You should've been there. Tom was there and he's definitely injured. You told me you were fit for this game. But you pull out just when I need you!"

He was still ranting about being let down when the final whistle sounded and the two weary teams trooped off the pitch. Although anyone else would have blamed the goalkeeper for the mistake that led to the equalizer, Ivan Jones was still furious with Joe.

"Unless you learn to carry on and play a whole game without dropping out, I won't have you in my team. There's always something wrong with you. You're never completely fit and healthy."

As he said this, the coach reached out and suddenly ripped the sticking plaster off Joe's thigh. "Ouch!" Joe yelled. But Ivan Jones ignored his cry of pain. Dramatically, he pointed at Joe's leg and yelled "So where are the bite marks, Joe? Show me! There's not a mark on you!"

"I'm a quick healer," Joe replied immediately.

"I just don't believe you, Joe," the coach carried on, not believing a word of what he'd heard. "And I can't have people I don't trust on my team."

"Joe's not lying, Mr Jones," cried Amy who'd watched everything. "That dog did bite him and Joe's always brave about injuries. He just gets a lot of them, that's all."

Joe shot Amy a grateful but guilty glance. He guessed Ivan Jones wouldn't like her interrupting and he was right.

"You keep out of this, girl," he told her. Then he added: "I notice you didn't do so well in the second half. Slowed down didn't you?"

Amy turned away, disgusted by the coach's attitude. "Come on, Joe," she said softly. "Let's go home. Nobody wants us here."

Chapter Seven

Next day, at the end of school, Amy limped over to Joe and said "Let's go to the park. I want to ask you something."

Joe raised an eyebrow.

"Come on. But don't go too fast. My leg still aches after that maniac kicked me. The bruise makes a rainbow look boring! You seem to be OK, though."

"Yeah, not bad," he nodded. "But I wouldn't tell Ivan Jones that. He doesn't believe anything I say."

When they reached Shipton Park, the playground was deserted. Amy swayed to and fro on a swing. "You promised to tell me why you don't trust coaches, remember?" she said, suddenly. Joe nodded, though he wished she'd forgotten. "So tell me now, Joe. I might feel the same myself."

Joe leaned against the swing and was silent for a moment. "The first coach I had was my dad," he suddenly blurted out. "He was always putting me down, saying I lacked something in my game though he never said just what it was. The thing is," he continued, "he's the coach for the under 14's. He reckons that he can't have favourites, so he ignores me and never notices what I do.

It's all his team and his reputation. I never get praise for playing well. He'd only use me in a team if he was really desperate, but I'd just as quickly get dropped the next week. So, I've learnt that coaches can't be trusted. I get my own back on them by inventing injuries and going off when I've scored. If I'm hurt people notice – my parents notice – they talk to me and comment on the game."

Amy sighed. "Yes, but the team's important too, Joe. You're not just letting the coach down when you drop out."

"Yes, I suppose you're right." Joe nodded.

Neither of them knew that someone else was watching them at that moment. Miss Tolley, walking through the park on her way home, had spotted them. Joe hadn't been wearing plasters or bandages this week and he had seemed happier. Now, Miss Tolley could guess why. She was sure Amy was having a good influence on him and she was glad to see signs of a friendship. As they walked towards the gate, she noticed that Amy was still limping as she had done all day. It was odd, now that Joe was fully fit, Amy was the injured one!

"Listen, Joe, you've got to forget about the past and play brilliantly on Sunday," Amy said as they stood outside her house. "You were brave to play when you were injured. Now you can let old Ivan Jones see how brilliant you are when you're fit."

"I don't think I'm his favourite player," Joe said. "He probably won't pick me."

"If he doesn't, I'll make the rest of the team go on strike!" Amy said. She was smiling but she meant every word.

Chapter Eight

The following Sunday, the Swifts were playing Tingley Typhoons, who always boasted that they could blow any opposition away. They looked capable of it, too – they were a big, strong-looking side.

"Hello," Ivan Jones said to Joe when he arrived. "I've decided to let you play today. This is your final chance to prove to me that you are fully fit and committed to the team. Are you ready for this?"

"Yes, Mr Jones," Joe replied.

"Good because we're down to the bare bones today. Tom and Amy are both out with knocks. So you stay out of trouble. Typhoon's big central defender can mix it a bit so don't lose sight of him. Anyway, you've got pace and he hasn't. Give it all you've got."

But it was Amy's final words that Joe took on to the pitch with him. "Just show them, Joe," she said as she stood on the touchline. "I know you can do it. Win it for us."

"Do my best," he said. But it was some time before he even touched the ball as the Typhoons swept down on the Swifts' goal.

"Keep 'em out, boys!" Ivan Jones kept yelling and, somehow, they did. Yet the siege went on

and on as the Swifts were simply penned in their own half. Joe even thought of dropping back to help out. Maybe the coach would have liked that, but Joe knew he had to be ready  for any breakaway chance. He was convinced that he was the only striker who could score for the Swifts.

Then, when the ball unexpectedly reached him from a misplaced pass, Joe moved fast. All the same, he wasn't quite fast enough to outwit the big central defender. The Typhoon player mowed Joe down with one lunge. The ref blew for the foul and anxiously asked Joe if he was all right.

"Yeah, no problem," Joe replied – and he meant it. He really had come out of the tackle unscathed. But his opponent hadn't. Amazingly, that solid, rock-like defender had fallen badly and damaged his knee on the hard pitch. A few minutes later he limped off the pitch and out of the match altogether.

Joe sensed his luck had changed completely. He felt he would succeed, whatever he tried.

He did. Whenever he had the ball, he skipped away from trouble. His first touch was perfect, his dribbling inspired, his pace electric. He scored his first goal after ten minutes and his second two minutes from the end. That was wonderful timing and the Swifts held on to win 2–1. Joe's team-mates applauded him off the pitch.

"Terrific, you're a star!" said Ivan Jones, slapping him on the back. But it was the hug from Amy that pleased Joe the most.

Read more of Michael Hardcastle's soccer stories:

SOCCER SECRET

Tom is a brilliant striker and he likes nothing better than
boasting about all the goals he scores.
What he doesn't know is that his cousin, Alan,
is good at football too – as a goalie.
When will Alan get the recognition he deserves,
without upsetting Tom?

STRIKER'S BOOTS

Sean has waited for weeks to get a place in the school
soccer team. He's almost given up hope when the coach
picks him at last! Then disaster strikes. He's forgotten
his boots. How can he play? This could be his big chance,
but how on earth can he score goals in bare feet?

RIVALS UNITED

When East End's star striker defects to the West End
team, his team-mates can't believe it. Just what does
David think he's playing at? Then there's a local derby
when the two teams meet. The winning team
could be promoted to league status,
but where do David's loyalties lie?

For more information about Mega Stars, write to:
The Sales Department, Macdonald Young Books,
61 Western Road, Hove, East Sussex BN3 1JD